BUILT for LOVE

A POWERFUL LOOK AT THE SOURCE OF LOVE
AND HOW WE CAN LOVE OTHERS WELL

CASANDRA MERRITT

Built for Love: A Powerful Look at the Source of Love and How We Can Love Others Well

Book Creation and Design
DHBonner Virtual Solutions, LLC
www.dhbonner.net

Printed in the United States of America

I want to dedicate this book to all my family and friends; love covers an abundance. When life challenges you, always remember, love never fails.

Table of Contents

Introduction   vii

1. We're Built for Love   1
2. Eros Love: Don't Be Stupid About
   Cupid   7
3. Storge Love: A Natural Bond   19
4. Phileo Love: Be Devoted to One
   Another   31
5. Agape Love: Foundational and
   Unconditional   37
6. Love has a Language   45
7. Commitment, Longevity, and Stability   53
8. Feelings vs. Holy Spirit as Indicator   61
9. The Fullness of Love   77
10. Take it Step by Step   89

   About the Author   101
   Bibliography   103

Introduction

I am passionate about the subject of love! As a therapist, I work with people of different ages and backgrounds, but something they each have in common in one way or another revolves around this thing called *love*.

Love is a big deal! It's a part of all our lives in various forms and countless ways. Each. And. Every. Day. It profoundly affects us, and how we receive and give love significantly affects others. Something this essential in our lives is worth our time and attention to examine and learn more about, don't you think?

To help you get the most out of this book, I will invite you at the end of each chapter to pause and answer specific questions about love and how it pertains to you. We all need more pauses in our life–a moment or two to digest what we're learning and reflect on it. In this way, you will be able to soak up and apply what this book has for you on the subject of love.

The term "love" is so generically thrown around, and we may naturally first think of it in romantic terms, but it's much more. It was the Greeks who categorized love into various types, the main ones being these four: *Eros, Storge, Phileo,* and *Agape.* In the following chapters, we'll explore each one and learn what they mean by definition and how they play out practically and spiritually in our lives.

By the way, it's not by chance you have this book in your hands. I believe God has led you to it, and I pray he will use it in your life in helpful, encouraging, and profitable ways. May you find insight and wisdom in these pages. I hope my words help open your eyes and heart to the power and realities of love.

That is my prayer for you!

I love you,
Casandra

Chapter 1

We're Built for Love

I t's not uncommon to question people's love for us. A friend cancels our lunch date for the second time, and we question whether we matter to her. Our boyfriend doesn't return our text, though we know he saw it, and we wonder if his feelings for us are waning. Our teenager tells us he can't wait to leave the nest and get out of the house, and we feel rejected. We don't receive "likes" on our social media posts and feel unsupported or unaccepted.

These things can be challenging to navigate in a healthy way, yet it doesn't change the fact that we're built for love in the context of relationships.

As you read this book, you will notice that I've included some bible verses in most chapters as I point to

God as the source of love, though I'm aware that Scripture is more relevant for the believer than the believer non-believer. If you're not a Christian, these scriptures may not affect you in the same way as they would a believer; however, I implore you to read them with an open mind and heart.

No matter where we find ourselves spiritually, we have all been created with the instinct to love, and the verses and other quotes I include speak to that claim. I believe they are relevant to all our lives and the relationships we have or want to have with others.

It doesn't matter if you're an introvert or extrovert, male or female, five or one hundred and five. Each of us was made to be in relationship with others and experience love. We experience love through our familial and romantic relationships, friendships, and, most importantly, our relationship with God. In fact, it's only by having a relationship with Christ that we can effectively and rightly love others. That may seem like the boldest of statements, but it's true. Why? Because God is not only the inventor of love, but the Bible tells us that he *is* love! He built (created) us out of love and for love.

Scripture tells us that we were carefully and wonderfully made by a loving God (Psalm 139). Throughout the Bible, we are told and shown that he loves us (John 3:16). We are also commanded to love others (1 John 4:7), and we're told we have the ability to love because of Jesus (1 John 1:9). The great news is, God doesn't leave us in the dark as to how we are to love. We don't have to figure out for ourselves what it means to love others. We've been given a clear and multi-faceted picture of what love is meant to look like from God himself. We will go over this in greater detail in the chapters to follow, but here's an introduction:

> Love endures with patience *and* serenity, love is kind *and* thoughtful, and is not jealous *or* envious; love does not brag and is not proud *or* arrogant. It is not rude; it is not self-seeking, it is not provoked [nor overly sensitive and easily angered]; it does not take into account a wrong *endured*. It does not rejoice at injustice, but rejoices with the truth [when right and truth prevail]. Love bears all things [regardless of what comes], believes all things [looking for the best in each one], hopes all things [remaining steadfast during difficult times], endures all things [without weakening].

-1 Corinthians 13:4-7 AMP

Isn't that amazing? Isn't it beautiful? Doesn't that sound like mature, fulfilling love? It's a tall order, though, right? It may seem impossible to love and be loved in those ways, but actually, it is possible. Yet, we can't love like that in our own power or strength. We may have the instinct to love, but when that love has not been regenerated through Christ, we can't give the authentic love that wants to ooze out of us because it doesn't know how to do it.

Our fallback is romantic love. And we can't even receive that kind of love to the fullest without receiving Jesus and accepting his unconditional love for us.

It gets down to this: We have a choice whether or not we will obey God's command and love others as he intended. We also have a choice whether or not we will accept the love he has for us through Jesus Christ, which can open up possibilities (positive or negative) or shut them down. When we receive Christ, we are given the Holy Spirit. His job is to help, guide, counsel, and convict us. His presence is vital to help us navigate *Eros, Storge, Phileo,* and *Agape* love.

As we explore these, we will receive a fuller picture of what love truly means and what we're signing up for or rejecting when it comes to love. Not all types of love carry the same amount of weight. But there is one where we are to put our greatest attention, and when we do, the others become better, fuller... enhanced.

We are wise to learn about these loves and discern how much weight to give each type and the importance of incorporating one, in particular, into all the others.

Chapter 2

Eros Love: Don't Be Stupid About Cupid

We're all familiar with the winged, cherub-like images of artists' renditions of Cupid. If he's wearing any clothes at all, it's usually a simple pair of underwear. He's depicted hovering in mid-air, bow and arrow in hand. Often the tip of his arrow is in the shape of a heart, and he's taking aim, ready to "inflict" love on his subject! He looks so cute and innocent, but there's more to his origin. In classical mythology, Cupid is the god of Desire, symbolizing attraction and romantic love. His counterpart in Greek mythology is Eros (pronounced "EHR-ōs"), where we get the term "Eros Love."

The term Eros refers to erotic love, which Merriam-Webster's Dictionary defines as (in addition to "the god of erotic love") "...the sum of life-preserving instincts that are manifested as impulses to gratify basic needs...." Simply put, Eros encompasses sex, desire, and attraction. It's the basic stuff of a good Harlequin Romance novel or romantic comedy movie. Humans are drawn to Eros Love and instinctively want to experience it. It's natural and not wrong in its intended purpose within the context of marriage.

Still, it's easy to pollute and distort Eros if we don't see it for what it is and understand our relationship with it or when we give this form of love more power in our lives than it was meant to have.

The word "love" is generically thrown around and we grow up associating it mostly with romance because that's what society champions–in songs, movies, advertisements, and more. But there is so much more to the fullness of love than Eros! And we can't even give this kind of love to others in a proper way without a different type of love accompanying it.

Feeling Twitterpated?

In perhaps its purest form, we first experience Eros Love as young as childhood. It doesn't take long before, as a little boy or girl, we find ourselves drawn to someone–

perhaps a fellow student at school, our friend's older sibling, or maybe the girl or boy next door. In the 1942 cartoon, *Bambi,* Disney introduces us to the term "twitterpated," meaning being smitten with a love interest.

When we're young and have these feelings, we're told we have a crush on someone or we're experiencing "puppy love." We may be compelled to write our love interest a note declaring our feelings or even try and make known our affection for our crush by showing off somehow or slugging the person in the arm as a misguided way of flirting! Maybe we pick our love interest to be on our team during recess to communicate our devotion to them.

As we get a little older–usually in our teen years–and look back on the first real relationship where we experienced Eros, we give it the title of "first love," no matter how romantic it actually was or to what degree we experienced intimacy. We may have experienced "butterflies in our stomach" whenever we saw the person. We may have held hands or kissed. Perhaps we went "all the way" with that person.

At the time, and maybe for years afterward, we thought we were in love, and we may look back at that experience of "first love" with great fondness if we remember it in a favorable light. Or there may be some mixed feelings that come with our reminiscing. Regardless, the fact remains Eros Love evokes strong emotions.

No matter how it turned out for us, at least at the beginning, Eros Love is exciting and fun! Nothing is as enticing to us as attracting love and we were built for love even in this way. We all want to experience romantic love, and the truth is God created it and wired us to respond to it. Romantic love between two people in a committed marriage relationship should be beautiful and can be productive (after all, it's through our sexual desire, generally, that babies are made)!

Eros, however, is based on feelings and emotions, which can be both fleeting and deceiving, even within marriage. So, while Eros can be wonderful and not wrong in and of itself, it falls short of being a complete picture of love. The love we were built for is bigger and deeper. Eros just isn't enough to satisfy on its own because it is based on emotions and desires and these things change.

We love the emotional, though, don't we? Eros Love makes for exciting television, movies, music videos, and books. And Eros is everywhere! Billy Graham is quoted to have said, *"Society has become so obsessed with sex that it seeps from all the pores of our national life."* Those are such true words! As a society, it seems sex is on the forefront of our minds. This is the reason why the marketing world uses the phrase "sex sells." We're drawn to it and what it seems to represent.

When we experience Eros Love firsthand, it makes us feel alive in a sensual way. Unfortunately, the examples our culture commonly feeds us (and we feed ourselves) of Eros Love do not always help us to have a right and healthy view of sex and romantic love. When we give Eros too much of ourselves—when we allow it to take over our minds and choices—we can elevate it to a place of most importance in our lives. When that happens, we distort it and overestimate its value.

Sheri's Story

Twenty-seven-year-old Sheri liked to date, and ever since high school, she had a series of boyfriends, each lasting anywhere from several months to a year. One day, a few months after she and her latest boyfriend broke up, she noticed Anthony, a new guy at work. He was tall and muscular, and she liked the way he dressed. She was also attracted to his gorgeous smile and his musky cologne.

Anthony had some serious sex appeal! Though she knew very little about him, she began fantasizing about him based on his appearance. She made up scenarios in her head about the life and sex they could have together. It wasn't long before the two began dating. After a few dates, Sheri realized that she and Anthony had different values and interests, but she liked the way he treated her and how he made her feel special, so she continued to date him.

Though she knew their relationship would not lead to marriage, her physical (sexual) attraction for him kept her interested. Their union, however, had nothing to do with the Spirit. She bonded with Anthony on a physical level, placing the sensations she received from him at the highest level. As a result, she gave away a part of herself to him for nothing more than a fleeting relationship based on feelings. It wasn't long before their Eros Love for one another waned.

Since their relationship was based on Eros and nothing deeper followed or was at the foundation, there wasn't enough between them to sustain the relationship. So, four months later, they broke up and went their separate ways.

As Sheri reflected over their time together, she was left with some regrets. She wished she had been more careful to see the relationship for what it was and end it earlier. In retrospect, she felt she wasted some precious time and, more importantly, gave away part of herself to a man who was not her husband and never would be.

You Can Make a Wise Choice

Let us not fall into a trap like Sheri and suffer the consequences of regrets and more! We can be attracted to someone without allowing the relationship to go "there." It all starts with what we allow our minds to entertain and dwell on. If you find yourself in a situation like Sheri, ask yourself, "Have I internally, mentally crossed a boundary?" If so, you have a choice. You can allow yourself to believe it's harmless and continue to fantasize, or you can exercise self-control and keep yourself in check.

I'm not saying it's easy, but "renewing your mind," as Romans 12:2 tells us, is worth the effort, and the Holy Spirit can help you. Just ask in faith!

If you find yourself in a situation where you're tempted to give into someone's flattering pursuit of you, or you have a mutual sexual desire for each other outside of marriage, and you know it's not right (whether or not anyone ever finds out), do yourself a favor and leave the situation and do it quickly! So, you know the story in the Bible about Potiphar's wife? She tried to seduce Joseph, her husband's right-hand man. Joseph could have easily given in to her and enjoyed himself, but he knew being with his boss's wife was wrong. (By the way, whoever says the Bible is boring, hasn't read it!)

Instead of trying to fool himself that he was strong enough to resist temptation, Joseph did the wisest thing: he fled! He didn't hang around to reason with her, but he got himself the heck outta there! Ultimately, God honored Joseph for his choice and rewarded him for his faithfulness in this and many other areas.

No matter where we find ourselves within Eros Love, we must remember that we can invite God into it. He invented sex, after all! He created us with natural desires for sex–to procreate, to bond with our spouse in a special way, and for enjoyment. We humans, however, have polluted God's intent for sex. Some of us have experienced abuse and must understand that we don't need to live in a victim mindset or be doomed to a generational curse.

If your parent had an affair, you're not destined to do the same. If there is an abuser in your line, you're not destined to be an abuser as if you have an "abuser gene." God is faithful to free and cleanse us from our past and any generational sin. The way to live free is to have a relationship with God and spend time in his presence, allowing him to redeem and heal. We don't need to give in to our unnatural inclinations and we are wise to recognize Satan's ploys to get us off track with what we know is right.

For example, I was once molested by a female and then years later, a masculine woman came on to me. I told her that "I don't get down like that" and that I was married... to a man. She fully understood and was gracious, but because I knew what had happened to me when I was young, I felt as if the woman's *spirit* was familiar with something that took place in my life and sought to take advantage of it. I say this because I had not put out a vibe as to any interest in her romantically. Eros is important and powerful, but it needs to know its place. We don't have to give in to its distortions when they present themselves. If and when we do, know this: God knows our thoughts, temptations, and desires. We can be honest with him, and if we make a wrong choice when it comes to our sexuality, we can find grace in Christ who redeems and restores.

Before I wrap up this chapter on Eros Love, I want to take this idea of physical attraction in a direction that includes more than just sex, though I admit it pushes the definition of "Eros." Still, let me just say that if we're not careful, we can have an attraction (or lust) for other things besides a human being. Maybe you're not struggling with sex, but you're attracted to shopping, eating, gaining success, making money, or something else to the point of over-indulgence. These things, along with sexual pursuits, can easily become idols when they're pursued, essentially, as "lovers."

For example, the Bible doesn't say that money is the root of all evil. It says *the love of money* is the root of all evil. Be careful with what and how you love. We're built to love people and use things, not the other way around!

Pause and Ask Yourself:

- When I look back on my dating relationships, was Eros Love the main focus?

- Did I hold onto a relationship or keep it going longer than I should have because I made my romantic feelings for them the main thing? If so, what was the result?

- What steps can I take next time to help me guard against a wrong focus?

- Do I have a "love" attraction toward something other than a person? What is it? How does that play out in my life?

- If you're currently in a committed, romantic relationship, ask yourself: What do I love about this person? And, is my love based primarily on my feelings and our romantic involvement, or is there more to it?

—♥—

Action Step: Take a few moments to list what you believe is critical to have in a committed, romantic relationship. Pray and ask God to help you make the right choices as you navigate an Eros Love relationship you are currently in (married or not). Then, confess anything the Holy Spirit convicts you of in this area.

Prayer: *Thank you, God, for Eros Love. You desire that my love life in the areas of sex, desire, and attraction is pure and unselfish. Help me to enjoy it freely but within the confines of your purposes. Also, thank you for your forgiveness, grace, and fresh beginnings. Amen.*

17

Chapter 3

Storge Love: A Natural Bond

Storge (pronounced "STOR-ghay") is an Ancient Greek word referring, in part, to the first love we experience beginning the moment we are born into a family or adopted into one. It is a familial and instinctive love. It's marked by affection and care. In the animal kingdom, creatures instinctively know how to care for their young, but human parents are capable of even more. Humans are prone to love their offspring in practical *and* emotional ways, and this natural bond continues through our entire lives.

The trust of love starts with our parents and the people in our environment. Parents are the ones who introduced us to love. A baby is born, and the family rejoices. The infant is swaddled and fed by a devoted parent as they give them eye contact and hold them affectionately and lovingly–at least that is the most natural scenario. Other family members also interact with the baby, supplying more smiles, tender words, and touches. Parents change diapers, provide a safe place for the baby to sleep, and ensure their needs are met. They share a natural bond and affection from day one, and day by day, as the baby grows and is nurtured, he responds to and reciprocates his parents' love. Remember, we were born to love... and to be loved!

This plays out in various ways, and one example can be found between fathers and daughters. It's not uncommon to see little girls who have the presence of a loving father at home experience a sense of security that is cultivated by his interaction and appropriate affection toward them. When a father isn't around, a form of violation of love occurs, whether that child (male or female) is aware of it or not. The father's presence and positive attention tells the child they're accepted; when we feel accepted, we feel loved. At a young age, this takes root in our lives, positively or negatively.

While Eros, or romantic love, is an integral part of a healthy marriage between a husband and wife, Storge also plays a role. As a man and woman share experiences and "do" life together by raising kids, carrying out family and household responsibilities, supporting one another, and functioning as a family unit, ideally, they experience a partnership marked by affection, compassion, and acceptance. It's an unforced, natural, bonding love—a love for which we were built.

Storge Love is also shared between siblings on some level, even when sibling rivalry exists. It's a devoted love, and, in the case of siblings, the Bible addresses this with the expectation that we, indeed, possess it. When the Apostle Paul wrote the book of Romans, he gave an example of how the brethren, Christians, were to treat one another.

> "Be devoted to one another with [authentic] brotherly affection [as members of one family], give preference to one another in honor;...." -Romans 12:10

He gives this example because Storge Love is natural. His readers then *and now* would understand what he meant because we all experience to some degree familial love in our lives. It's the meaning behind the saying, "Blood is thicker than water." The assumption is the relationships and loyalties that are part of the family dynamic are our strongest and most important ones. Paul uses the example of the bond we share with a family member (in this case a brother) to underscore the way we are to love those who are brothers and sisters in the Christian faith. Loving a *brother or sister in Christ*—a fellow believer—may not be natural in the same sense as Storge Love, but it is similar.

It's also possible on the deepest of levels because of Agape Love, which I will explain in detail in Chapter Five. Storge, in and of itself, however, is limited.

So, at its best, Storge Love is a natural, beautiful, and strong bond. The love between two siblings, the tender affection between a parent and their child—these are the relationships we all want to experience and enjoy, and most people do to one degree or another. But there is, of course, a more complicated side of these familial relationships that is less than "beautiful." You may not need to look any further than your own life to see that familial love is imperfect.

Perhaps you would say that you love your adolescent son, but his disobedient choices have caused you to no longer trust him, creating tension in your relationship. Or maybe you would say that you love your sister, but because you were hurt by something she said two months ago, you've allowed a wall to go up between you. Tumultuous relationships don't happen in every family, but they're not uncommon, and they're nothing new. They've been around since the beginning!

Family Dysfunction in History

We're given examples of unhealthy familial relationships in several chapters of the book of Genesis in the Old Testament. Take Cain and Abel. Though the Bible doesn't tell us specifically, the common interpretation of why Cain killed Abel was a typical cause of sibling rivalry: jealousy. Later in Scripture, we see a dysfunctional family in Isaac and Rebekah when we're told that Isaac favored their son, Esau, and Rebekah favored Jacob. Parents playing favorites is never healthy!

With Rebekah's help, Jacob cheats Esau out of his birthright, which, as you can imagine, sets in motion sibling rivalry, causing Jacob to flee the family to protect himself from the wrath of his brother. Then, when Jacob has a family of his own, more dysfunction plays out. His ten eldest sons throw their younger brother Joseph into a pit and sell him into slavery!

What caused them to do such a thing? Jealousy. It strangles affection. Joseph was his father's favorite, and that drove his older brothers nuts!

See? The bond of Storge Love is strong, but it isn't

enough. Like Eros, it can be a fickle love. It's incomplete when it stands alone. As with Eros Love, there are wonderful things about it, but it is lacking. In some cases, a father or mother deserts their child by leaving the family unit and not remaining an integral part of the child's life. When this happens, the bond of Storge is damaged and, often, is as absent as the parent who left.

Perhaps those real-life stories in the Bible were given to us as a warning and a reminder that God can handle our dysfunction. Not surprised by it, he's well aware of our sinful nature as humans. Still, we can and should come to him for guidance, help, and forgiveness and be willing to accept and respond favorably to his correction and discipline. He can redeem dysfunction! Remember, he built us for love.

If you're a parent, then you know how natural it is to possess Storge Love (a sincere familial love) for your child, yet still provoke them to wrath from time to time! In the Bible, we are told to "Train up a child in the way he should go..." (Proverbs 22:6). As parents, we are the primary ones to carry this out, and as we do, we are following the example of our Heavenly Father. Hebrews 12:6 says, "For the Lord disciplines and corrects those whom He loves, And He punishes every son whom He receives and welcomes [to His heart]."

One act of loving our children is to follow Christ's example and discipline them. But fathers (and mothers) are instructed by God to not behave in a way toward their children that would cause them to feel intensely frustrated. Ephesians 6:4 (AMP) tells us:

Fathers, do not provoke your children to anger [do not exasperate them to the point of resentment with demands that are trivial or unreasonable or humiliating or abusive; nor by showing favoritism or indifference to any of them], but bring them up [tenderly, with lovingkindness] in the discipline and instruction of the Lord.

As parents, we are obligated to control our own emotions as we strive to raise our children correctly through fair and appropriate discipline and loving correction. But we all know that children naturally do not like to be disciplined (by either parent), yet if we neglect to do so, we ultimately fail them and disobey God who has given us the gift and responsibility of caring for our children in the first place. How and when we discipline our children should be motivated by our sincere love for them paired with our love for God and not done out of anger or frustration.

Still, even when we get it right, children of all ages will sometimes feel like our love isn't what they want it to be no matter how fair and even merciful we are toward them in our discipline. So, when we correct them, they may feel like we don't love them. Yet, in its purest form, we correct or punish *because* of our love for them. Though they may not understand that at the moment, ideally, as they mature, they will have an accurate understanding and appreciation of our discipline. Even if they don't, one way we love them as parents is through fair and loving correction.

The added reality to all this, unfortunately, however, is that we are human, and we won't always carry out our parental duties perfectly, especially when it comes to how we handle discipline. This is yet another way that Storage Love is present and important but not complete.

Perhaps because Storge Love is natural and built into our lives from birth to the grave, it is easy to take it for granted. Yet Storge Love requires effort on our part in order to keep it healthy or, if it is unhealthy, to bring our familial relationships to a healthy place. We must regularly practice forgiveness, patience, compassion, understanding, and more with our family members if these relationships are to flourish.

Once again, there is another love that must accompany it for Storge to be most effective! Storge will only take us so far in our familial relationships.

Pause and Ask Yourself:

- In what ways does Storge Love manifest itself in my life? What do I appreciate about my family?

- How well am I loving my parents, siblings, and extended family members? How might I do better in showing my love?

- Is there someone in my family I have a grudge against or who holds a grudge against me? How can I play a part in bringing peace and healing to this situation?

- Have I been playing favorites with any of my children? How can I be fairer?

Action Step: If you're a parent and find yourself in a season of losing your cool with your kid(s), be intentional about improving in this area–for their sake and your own. Take one or more of these action steps:

- Reach out to someone you trust and ask them to keep you accountable for keeping your temper in check and disciplining appropriately. This may be humbling for you, but it's a loving action for your child's sake.

- If necessary, seek an experienced counselor to help you understand the root of any anger issues you may be dealing with.

- Admit to God where you have fallen short in this area and invite him into your struggle. You're forgiven, and he wants to help you! Remember: "God is our refuge and strength [mighty and impenetrable], A very present *and* well-proved help in trouble" (Psalm 46:1 AMP).

Prayer: *God, thank you for Storge Love. I am grateful for the family you have put in my life. None of us are perfect but help me to see each family member as you do and show love in a way that honors them and glorifies you. Amen.*

Chapter 4

Phileo Love: Be Devoted to One Another

The Ancient Greeks identified another kind of love we experience, this one between friends. Phileo Love (pronounced "Fil-EH-oh" or sometimes also called "Philia") is the love we have for those closest to us beyond our family. It's the love we have for our closest friends. And what a gift it is to have someone in our life who is a kindred spirit!

When a companion like that enters our life, we have more than a buddy. We have a confidante. Most of us would say we have friends at work, in our community, at school, at the gym, at church, and more, but we have a brotherly (or sisterly) affection and devotion for, perhaps, only a handful of friends in our life. These are the people we go deeper with.

When we were children, this may be the friend we hung out with most often. We played together, shared possessions, stuck up for one another, divulged our secrets to each other, and enjoyed giggling together! We may have fought from time to time, but we made up and would still call each other our "BFF."

Now, as we get older, our "Phileo Love" friendships may have the same makeup as when we were kids, but our sense of Phileo or devotion has grown to a deeper connection. This love is now shared with someone we lean on for support while they count on us to be there in their hour of need. We enjoy each other's company, and there is an ease about being together. Most of the time, on issues of prime importance to us, like morality and faith, we share a common ground and tend to be like-minded, but we also accept each other's differences. We trust each other, a sense of warmth and kindness is present, and we prioritize each other.

This is a picture of what Phileo Love often looks like, though it varies because no two relationships are the same. When all is going right in our friendships, we can see how we were built for love. But, when a friend betrays us, or we no longer share a close bond with a friend for some other reason, we can walk away from the relationship and feel justified. Why? Because, whether we admit it or not, some strings are attached to Phileo Love. It's not complete without Agape Love at its center.

There are some beautiful examples of Phileo Love in the Bible. These examples stand out because Agape Love was present within Phileo. (Hang on–you will learn about Agape Love in the next chapter!)

Friendships in the Bible

The Bible illustrates Phileo for us several times — in both the New and Old Testaments. We see it clearly in the relationship between David and Jonathan (1 Samuel 18:1). The Message version says it this way:

> ...By the time David had finished reporting to Saul, Jonathan was deeply impressed with David—an immediate bond was forged between them. He became totally committed to David. From that point on he would be David's number-one advocate and friend.

Later, David laments when Jonathan is killed and calls him his brother in 2 Samuel 1:26a (AMP): "I am distressed for you, my brother Jonathan; You have been a good friend to me. Your love toward me was more wonderful Than the love of women..."

Brother, yet not by blood. The two men were close friends with a kindred spirit bond. What a beautiful picture of Phileo Love!

Jesus enjoyed a Phileo Love friendship with Martha, Mary, and their brother Lazarus. When Lazarus died, Jesus wept, in part, most likely because his sisters were grieving, and it moved Jesus to tears to see them suffering in grief. (Of course, we know he wasn't weeping for Lazarus because he knew he would soon raise him from the dead!) Friends have compassion for each other, and we see this as Jesus is moved to tears.

We see another tender picture of Phileo Love in John 13:23 (NKJV) between Jesus and his disciple, John: *"Now there was leaning on Jesus' bosom one of His disciples, whom Jesus loved."* These days, for a number of reasons in many cultures, friends–especially men–don't usually show this type of outward, physical affection. Most likely, there is a concern that the affection will be misunderstood by the recipient or others who witnessed it. But strong affection and tenderness are part of Phileo or Brotherly Love, even when it is not demonstrated through physical touch. We feel it, and it may even show on our countenance even when we don't demonstrate it with a hug or some other form of physical contact.

Unlike Storge Love, Phileo is not built into our lives from day one of our existence. We are not born with Phileo Love in place because we do not come into this world with an automatic best friend from birth, at least one who is not a sibling. We must find, recognize, and nurture these friendships for Phileo Love to develop and thrive. Even then, there are no guarantees that our Brotherly/Sisterly Love relationship will always stay in place.

Friendships can ebb and flow. We may enjoy a season of a close friendship with someone, but then they move away, and we lose touch. Also, people change, situations change, and affections can change, and all these factors and more can alter a relationship. As with Eros and Storge, Phileo is not a perfect love, yet it is made stronger, richer, better, and more complete when Agape Love is the foundation.

Pause and Ask Yourself:

- Who is someone in my life that I share a Phileo Love?

- What is it about this person (or people, if there is more than one) that compels me to feel such affection and devotion toward them?

- Has there been someone I once shared Phileo Love with that I no longer do? Why is that? Is there something I need to forgive that person for or ask forgiveness from?

———•———

Action Step: You've Identified one or more people with whom you share a Phileo Love. Now, take a few minutes to let them know that you appreciate their friendship. Call, text, or send a handwritten letter and share specific reasons why you love them and what makes you grateful for your relationship.

Prayer: *Thank you, God, for Phileo Love. You've created us as relational beings and provided for my needs through the gift of friendship. Please help me to be a good friend to others. Amen.*

Chapter 5

Agape Love: Foundational and Unconditional

As I've highlighted Eros, Storge, and Phileo in the preceding chapters, I hope you recognized both the beauty of these loves and how they fall short in and of themselves. It's safe to say that most humans are happy to participate in these loves at some point in their lives (and throughout their lives), and they each provide a measure of enrichment and fulfillment. However, there is another love–a complete, immeasurable, no-strings-attached, and uncompromising love–that is never based on emotions, situations, or attractions.

This love is far superior to the other three, and for the other three to be all they can be, this love is required. I'm referring to Agape Love.

A simple, yet profound definition of Agape Love

(pronounced, uh-GAH-pay) can be found in a quote by Martin Luther King, Jr. He put it this way regarding how we are to love others:

> *Agape is disinterested love... Agape does not begin by discriminating between worthy and unworthy people, or any qualities people possess. It begins by loving others for their sakes... Therefore, agape makes no distinction between friend and enemy; it is directed toward both.*

Agape is: "God's perfect, unconditional love." It's an outpouring of who God is. Think of those words: Perfect and unconditional. That's God, the source of Agape Love. He's also holy, unchangeable, almighty, and 100% good, to name just a few more attributes. Agape Love seems impossible to grasp and overwhelmingly wonderful simultaneously — just like God himself! The Bible tells us, "...The one who does not love has not become acquainted with God [does not and never did know Him], for God is love. [He is the originator of love, and it is an enduring attribute of His nature.]" -1 John 4:8 (AMP).

This is Agape Love—the love God *is*, the love he has *for us*, and the love he wants us to *live out*, the love for which we were *built to experience and bestow to others*. This love is demonstrated through actions and is not based on feelings. It makes no distinctions. We see the ultimate example of this when we read John 3:16 (NIV): "For God so loved the world that he gave his one and only Son, that whoever believes in him shall not perish but have eternal life." Agape love is also sacrificial. It is undeserved and gracious. It's ongoing and never absent. And it's available through Christ.

Now think of the people in your life. There may be someone you know intimately and share an Eros Love relationship with. If you have a mother, father, sister, brother, etc., you experience a Storge Love. And, with your closest friends, you enjoy a Phileo Love. But are these loves complete? Are they perfect and unconditional? Unchangeable? Sacrificial? The honest answer must be "no." But when Agape Love enters the picture, it's a whole new ballgame! It enhances how we give and receive love because its motive is Christ himself.

Agape Love changes our lives and affects all the other loves for the better. When we have it, we not only enjoy it, but we can then pour it out onto others with the love we've been given through Jesus Christ.

Before we move forward and dive deeper into Agape Love, let's remind ourselves of some of what the

Bible has to say about the way we are to love and what love is to look like. To do this, reread the verses I highlighted back in chapter one, written below. Before you begin, take a deep breath and focus. Now, read slowly, allowing these words to soak in:

> Love endures with patience and serenity, love is kind and thoughtful, and is not jealous or envious; love does not brag and is not proud or arrogant. It is not rude; it is not self-seeking, it is not provoked [nor overly sensitive and easily angered]; it does not take into account a wrong endured. It does not rejoice at injustice, but rejoices with the truth [when right and truth prevail]. Love bears all things [regardless of what comes], believes all things [looking for the best in each one], hopes all things [remaining steadfast during difficult times], endures all things [without weakening].

> -1 Corinthians 13:4-7 AMP

Sometimes Love Calls for Limits

Did you notice that these verses begin with the phrase "Love endures" and end with "endures all things"? To *endure* means to suffer patiently or remain in existence. That's a hallmark attribute of Agape Love! This endurance is not based on how we feel or whether or not a person deserves it. God endures our mistakes and loves us no matter what. He is our example as to how we are to love others. Agape Love has no conditions because it "endures *all* things," even when it hurts, is inconvenient or annoying, or is unfair.

Agape Love is unconditional but let me say here that doesn't mean Agape Love doesn't have boundaries. Sometimes, love calls for limits and boundaries to be put in place for the sake of the person we love. We are to set these up without anger and resentment but with a sincere heart of wanting the best for the person and our relationship.

For example, in chapter three on Storge Love, we learned that disciplining our children is one way we love them as parents. As our babies become young kids and then grow older and become teenagers and then young adults, our love and commitment to them sometimes call for us to create healthy boundaries.

For instance, if your capable twenty-year-old does not go to school or work and spends his days playing video games in your basement, it's time to put some healthy boundaries in place! You are to love that "child" (a young adult) by making some demands on him, like *getting a job or attending school. Do these certain chores at home. Pay this much rent each month or help buy groceries.* Or, if your teenager is on drugs and pays for them by stealing from you, you're not loving him by looking the other way and allowing him to do it. You're demonstrating love for him when you put boundaries in place, even though it will make him mad.

Agape Love doesn't "endure all things" by doing nothing. Sometimes tough love is part of Agape Love. Neither Storge nor Agape Love means you live co-dependently. Agape love means you're devoted to the relationship and the person; you endure the pain you may suffer because of their choices and remain in relationship with them as far as it depends on you, but you set boundaries when that is what is needed.

This isn't always easy to navigate, and we may not always get it right, but love is patient and kind–not only to the person we are committed to loving but also as we love ourselves! By loving ourselves, I'm not saying that we prioritize ourselves above others, but rather that we have a healthy view of who we are according to who God says we are. This is based on his unconditional love for us and not on how loveable we are. Thank God for that!

The Key to Agape Love

Simply knowing what Agape Love looks like does not mean we will love that way. We must seek Christ. Even then, we will never "do" Agape perfectly because we are human, but we can receive the power and help we need to love with Agape Love when we know Christ and accept his love for us. That is the key. Once we accept his love and his Spirit is in us, we are regenerated. Regeneration is a "new birth," making us new creatures in Christ Jesus, and that's a game changer for all the other loves and for our life! For example, suppose my spirit has not been regenerated. In that case, I can't discern whether I'm being led to the person I have a natural attraction to by the Holy Spirit or by my own desires, which are not always trustworthy. There is nothing wrong with natural attraction and Eros Love, but we need Agape Love to be infused into it to make it what it should be. When Agape enters the picture, true love is experienced—our perspective changes.

Pause and Ask Yourself:

- Have I experienced Agape Love through Christ? (If you haven't and would like to, I

will walk you through how to receive Jesus
into your life and experience Agape Love
firsthand in Chapter Eight.)

- Do I wholeheartedly believe that God loves
  me with unconditional love? If so, how does
  that change the way I love others? How does
  that change the way I love and accept
  myself?

———⚘———

Action Step: Write out 1 Corinthians 13:4-7 in any
version of your choice and post it on your mirror, fridge,
car, or wherever you will see it and read it often. Let the
words of these verses soak in and remind you of the way
you are to best love others.

Prayer: *Thank you, God, for Agape Love! All other
loves pale in comparison. Help me to fully accept your
Agape Love and love others in a way that reflects your
unconditional love for me. Amen.*

Chapter 6

Love has a Language

In the book, *The 5 Love Languages: The Secret to Love That Lasts*, Gary Chapman, Ph.D., highlights the five main ways romantic partners express and experience love. These love languages not only play out in Eros Love but also in our Storge and Phileo Love relationships. They are good to keep in mind as we seek to love others with a robust, effective love and, at its foundation, Agape.

We may desire to experience and receive love in all five of these ways, but, according to Chapman, there is usually one or two of these "languages" that speak love to people the most.

The five love languages are:

Acts of Service
Receiving Gifts
Quality Time
Words of Affirmation
and Physical Touch.

We love others best when Agape is our focus and when we know the "language" of love that best communicates love to the person we have a relationship with. This means we need to ask the person how they like to be loved. Don't assume you already know! Hear it from them. If you are seeking to learn the best ways to love your young child (or an uncommunicative teenager!) for example, recognize that they may not be able to verbalize how they like receiving love. So, you will need to be a detective. Learn by watching how they respond to these different love languages. This should tell you what they value most, what speaks love to them. Identify your preferred language of love and then think through what others in your life prefer.

Do actions speak louder than words for you? Do you feel loved by your husband when he fills your car with gasoline and helps you fold the clothes? If you feel most loved when someone does something for you, then it may be that *Acts of Service* is probably your preferred love language.

Do you feel most loved when someone you're in a relationship with (spouse, child, sibling, friend) gives you a present? If you feel incredibly valued, cherished, and loved when this happens, *Receiving Gifts* is most likely your love language.

Maybe you feel love most when you have someone's undivided attention. This love language is called *Quality Time.* It doesn't mean the person loving you needs to hold your hand and look into your eyes, but when they show you somehow that you are the one they want to be with at the moment, you feel loved.

Perhaps you feel especially loved when someone with whom you're in a relationship speaks words of encouragement to you. They express in words that they appreciate you. If you feel loved when you feel affirmed by someone, your primary love language may be *Words of Affirmation.*

Another love language Chapman highlights is *Physical Touch.* If actions such as a desired hug, kiss, handholding, or friendly arm around your shoulders make you deeply feel loved, then Physical Touch may be the best way your mate, friend, or parent can express their love to you.

Of course, there is more to each of these love languages, and I encourage you to read Chapman's book, but this brief explanation should spark some idea of how you want to be loved and how you can best love the most important people in your life. With this knowledge and Agape Love, you will love well.

Ethan and Kendra's Story

Not long after Ethan and Kendra married, both began questioning their spouse's love for them. The issue arose when they were dating and engaged, but it only grew once they married. It all started with their birthdays. When Ethan's birthday came around, Kendra planned for weeks what she would buy him. She went all out, purchasing several gifts, wrapping them just right, and then hiding them around the house for Ethan to search for, like a treasure hunt on the morning of his birthday. She also invited friends over and threw a party that night to help them celebrate.

Ethan appreciated the thought and all her efforts, but he didn't really want to hunt for a bunch of presents or spend the evening with a crowd. He was hoping to go away for the weekend and have some uninterrupted time with just him and Kendra. He thought, "I wish she hadn't spent so much on all this stuff. We could have used those funds on an Airbnb rental. Doesn't she want to spend time with me?"

For Kendra's birthday, Ethan took her to a beautiful garden at a hotel overlooking the ocean. They sat side-by-side on Adirondack chairs for an hour, talking, sipping wine, and watching the sunset together. When the sun disappeared behind the horizon, he presented her with a small box. Inside was a handwritten note announcing his present: a special dinner at the upscale hotel's in-house restaurant. Kendra thanked her husband for the gift but felt disappointed. She thought, "Is this the best he could do? Doesn't he know I like jewelry and clothes? He didn't even take the time to wrap the box or invite some friends to help me celebrate. Doesn't he love me?"

Do you see what is happening here? Kendra was loving Ethan the way she liked to be loved–with the love language of *Receiving Gifts*. Ethan was loving Kendra in the way he most felt loved, with the love language of *Quality Time*. As a result, each person was left wanting. They felt let down, disappointed, and, at least briefly, questioned whether or not their partner truly loved them. If left to fester, this "small" issue could grow to be a bone of contention in their relationship. We love better when we dial in to how others best experience love and then love them in that way.

Note that sometimes, the way we want to be loved changes with our season of life. For instance, a young mom who used to want quality time above all else may now feel most loved with acts of service. At this time in her life, folding the laundry or watching the kids so she can nap may speak more love to her than taking her on a coffee date. For this reason, it's helpful occasionally to ask the person we love how they desire to be loved.

In order for Kendra and Ethan to move through their situation in a way that protects and promotes love for one another, they would be wise to look to 1 Corinthians 13, which is Agape Love in action. Loving through Agape means they will endure and work through this situation with patience and kindness. Agape Love is willing to put in the time and effort and work things out by sharing thoughts and feelings and listening. Agape Love is in it for the long haul. It shows up in conversations where the dialogue is not rude or self-seeking. It's not touchy, and it doesn't keep score. It is forgiving. It assumes the best about the other person. Agape Love puts the other person first, so even when our desires are not being perfectly met, it hopes for good things to come.

See how Agape Love and the five love languages identified by Dr. Chapman go hand-in-hand? Eros, Storge, and Phileo are present as well, but it is Agape enveloping them that produces a firm foundation. Agape is strong, consistent, determined, unshakeable, and victorious—seeking to love others in the most effective and unselfish ways with no strings attached. It's how we all desire in our core to be loved. It's how Christ loves us, whether we are aware of it or not.

Pause and Ask Yourself:

- What is my love language?

- Can I identify how my family members and friends experience love?

- How am I loving others in the way they receive it best?

- Is Agape Love the foundation for how I love others? If so, what does that look like?

Action Steps: You may think you know how those in your life best experience love, but don't assume–ask! Have a conversation with your husband, children, parents, friends, etc. Tell them about the Five Love Languages and discuss them together.

Prayer: *Lord, thank you for how you've made us—each person unique. Please help me to accept the people closest to me as they are and learn to love them effectively. Amen.*

Chapter 7

Commitment, Longevity, and Stability

As we think of the four types of love discussed in this book, we can see that our trust in love starts at birth, as highlighted in chapter three. This love builds and matures over time and extends to others in our Eros and Phileo relationships. However, unfortunately, many times, and to varying degrees, love is violated in one way or another. For instance, love can be violated through a broken trust which manifests itself in countless scenarios, including abandonment and abuse (emotional, physical, mental, spiritual, or sexual).

Love is also violated when we give away our physical "love" in a self-centered or misguided manner. Love is violated or at least polluted whenever we live a self-centered life in general. And when we don't forgive someone who wronged us, a violation of love happens on both sides—by the one who wronged us and our unforgiveness of their transgression or offense.

A Story to Consider

Love at its best includes commitment, longevity, and stability, but humans can distort those virtues. We see this in Luke 15:11-32, in the parable of the prodigal son. (Even if you are familiar with this passage, reread it in the Message Version.) This story has three leading players: the prodigal son, his older brother, and their father. Let's examine how commitment, longevity, and stability play out in each character.

The parable begins with the youngest son making a bold and audacious move. He tells his father that he wants his inheritance early. His father gives it to him, and, not surprisingly, the son takes his new, unearned wealth and skips town. He shows a lack of respect by asking for the money in the first place, but he also shows a lack of commitment to his father and family, not only because he moves away but because he leaves to live for his *own* pleasure and look after his *own* interests. In doing this, he violates Storge Love.

The son's indulgent lifestyle probably brings him

great pleasure for a while, but later he reaps the consequences of his careless, self-centered ways. He is undisciplined in how he lives and squanders his money. As a result, he struggles to survive, and, to make matters worse, the country where he is living has fallen on challenging economic times. This young man who was once rollin' in the dough and livin' the life is forced to find work. Apparently, the only job he can secure is taking care of pigs.

He is hungry and miserable. This reality gets him thinking *I should go back home.* He learns his lesson and is humbled, so he doesn't plan on returning to his father, moving back into his old room, playing Xbox, and ordering pizza on his dad's credit card. He plans to confess to his father that he has sinned against both him and God. He will admit that he no longer deserves to be considered his father's son and then ask him if he would put him on his payroll as a hired hand. The son's thought process shows he has experienced both longevity and stability growing up. He wouldn't have dared show his face back home unless he had.

Longevity, in this case, points to constancy. This son would have felt the stability of his father's love throughout childhood; this demonstrates that it's in the relationship for the long haul. It's not hot one minute and cold the next. It's not intermittent. It's lifelong.

The son would have also had stability in his growing up to come home under such circumstances—in this case, pointing to support and security. He probably would not have even shown his face back home if he didn't trust his father or felt insecure about his love.

His father's character plays out in how he greets his son. "When he was still a long way off, his father saw him" (Luke 15:20 AMP).

Was he on the lookout for him? Was he hoping one day he'd return? We have no idea how long the son was gone. It could have been months or possibly years. Love hopes all things, according to 1 Corinthians, so it's likely the father was doing more than just casually keeping an eye out; he was scanning the horizon, longing to see his boy again. The father wants the best for his son because he is a committed parent, even though his son violated his love with his actions. Still, the father knows that being out "there," living the life he was living, was not good for him. So, when the father finally sees him, he doesn't wait for the son to come crawling back. He runs to greet his boy and showers him with kisses and hugs.

What a picture of forgiveness! What a demonstration of grace, unmerited favor, and mercy, withholding deserved punishment. The father enthusiastically welcomes his son home despite his wrong actions and violation of love. The father demonstrates to his son where he stands in the relationship–he is in it for the long haul (longevity), offering his support and security (stability) by allowing his prodigal son to come home and celebrating his return. Wow!

Enter now, the older brother. He does not share his father's joy in his brother's return. The older brother is self-righteous. He is also resentful and jealous of his younger brother, who seemingly got away with being disrespectful, unfaithful, and selfish when he had remained committed to his father and doing what was right. This, too, is a violation of love and can be cyclical in relationships. Sibling rivalry in Storge relationships is extremely common, and we're not told in this parable if this violation of love was ever restored and redeemed. However, it's a realistic picture of what happens in relationships where unconditional love is not exercised. Both the younger brother and the older brother violated love, but the younger brother owned up to it.

This story in the Bible is an illustration for us. The father's character in the story remains a constant picture of God. He is the same yesterday, today, and forever (Hebrews 13:8), and the prodigal's father is committed to his son–his love is unconditional and not contingent on his actions. This love is limitless and beyond reason. This is Agape Love in action! This parable is meant to show God's unconditional love and encourage us. It is also a lesson on how we are to love others.

Pause and Ask Yourself:

- Which character can I most relate to in the Parable of the Prodigal Son?

- How have those virtues played out in my life where I have been the one to bestow them on others?

- How has commitment, longevity, and stability played out in my life where I have been the recipient?

- Have I committed a violation of love against anyone? If yes, how?

Action Steps: If you answered "yes" to the last question above, create a game plan to correct a wrong. It could be a "simple" violation, like impatience with someone in your family. Or it could be something much bigger.

Be brave and honest with yourself. Then, pray and ask God to help you make things right with that person as far as it depends on you. Remember, they may not forgive you, but that doesn't excuse you from admitting a wrong and seeking forgiveness.

Prayer: *Dear God, you are the ultimate father. The only perfect father there is! Thank you for your unconditional love for me. Help me to believe it and share it with others.*

Chapter 8

Feelings vs. Holy Spirit as Indicator

When God made us, he created us to feel and have emotions. We may experience various emotions on any given day, including sadness, anger, happiness, pride, excitement, moodiness, playfulness, frustration, fear, and many other feelings. In part, that is what makes us human. But when we allow our emotions to reign, we can get ourselves into trouble.

The heart of man (this phrase includes women) is not always a wise guide or barometer of reality. Mark 7:21-23 (NLT) says, "For it is from within, out of a person's heart, that evil thoughts come—sexual immorality, theft, murder, adultery, greed, malice, deceit, lewdness, envy, slander, arrogance and folly. All these evils come from inside and defile a person."

We don't always think and feel in a way that leads us to make the right decisions or promotes healthier thinking. We must keep our thoughts and feelings in check because out of them come actions that can be devastating to ourselves and others.

It Started with an Email...

Take Michael's situation, for example. When he received an email from his sister that he didn't like, he was immediately *upset* and *irritated*. As he read through it, he felt like his sister was using a "tone," putting him on the *defensive*. He assumed his sister was judging him for something he did.

He reread the email twice, and both times it made his blood boil! So, out of *anger*, he quickly responded by sending an email of his own to defend himself.

Michael's words back to his sister were sharp and accusatory. When she read his response, she felt *hurt* and *misunderstood*. Because of this exchange over email, both siblings kept their distance from each other for nearly a year. A violation of their Storge Love took place, and their relationship became strained. It would take much effort and forgiveness to repair the damage so they could enjoy a healthy relationship once again, and they lost precious time together. Perhaps his sister was judging him with her comments, but if Michael had kept his feelings in check and assumed the best until he spoke with her, a much more positive outcome could have been the result.

Though it was right for him to express his feelings if he had called his sister (instead of communicating over text), expressed his feelings in a softer, less accusatory way, and invited a conversation, it's likely they both would have gained clarity and perspective and avoided this unfortunate and damaging conflict. A conversation done in love, even when we're feeling upset, makes it possible to reach an understanding that is helpful and healthy instead of rude and defensive and, therefore, damaging.

This story illustrates how—if we don't keep them in check—our feelings can get the better of us and wreak havoc in our relationships. Emotions can have too much power if we let them. They can lead to inaccurate or unfair assumptions, overtaking our common sense, morals, and convictions. They can blind us to or distort reality. They can also build a wall of unforgiveness and keep it erect for much too long. Dr. Gary Chapman underscores this truth.

Forgiveness is not a feeling; it is a commitment. It is a choice to show mercy, not to hold the offense up against the offender. Forgiveness is an expression of love.

When we focus on our feelings and nurse them, we will see this play out in Eros Love, even if we never thought we would follow through with our feelings. Their power, if we let them, can take over. When that happens, we may choose to have sex with someone other than a spouse. After all, we've already gone there in our minds and rehearsed it, if you will. If that person makes us feel good and allows us to give in to our romantic feelings toward them, we will cross a line and become ensnared in a damaging relationship.

We will also justify cheating on our spouse or significant other when we focus on our dissatisfaction in the relationship instead of focusing on commitment, longevity, and stability. So often, allowing our feelings to govern us will result in actions that will carry unfavorable consequences! This happens if our spirit has not been regenerated by the Holy Spirit. We are not able to discern if we're being led to someone romantically through the Spirit or our natural attraction.

Let's be clear. I am not saying we are to deny our

feelings. We need to recognize and acknowledge them, but that doesn't mean we should act on them. Instead, let's speak truth to feelings and learn to control how we respond or react to them! We choose to walk down a dangerous and dysfunctional path when we allow our feelings to be an indicator of how we will love or be loved.

The Gift that Keeps Giving: Holy Spirit

Remember, the source of love is Christ. He is the originator, the creator. He IS love! And his unconditional love for us provides a way for us to love others with Agape Love, which goes far beyond Eros, Storge, and Phileo. Remember, we were built for love. It was by God's design.

In addition to being our source of love, Christ is our example of love by how he lived and why he died. (He died for you and me but didn't stay dead —he rose from the grave!) When we accept Jesus into our lives, the Bible tells us we receive the Holy Spirit. The Spirit's role in our life is to give us an understanding of God's Word and to help, guide, counsel, and encourage us, among other things. There is so much to say about the role of the Holy Spirit that I would need to write a whole other book to explain it adequately! But for now, know this: When we believe in Christ, we are given the gift of the Holy Spirit as written in Romans 5:5 (NIV),

And hope does not put us to shame, because God's love has been poured out into our hearts through the Holy Spirit, who has been given to us."

When we have the Holy Spirit, we are given access to an immeasurable treasure! We can tune into his guidance and draw from the power he gives us to love others with Agape Love. Then we no longer need to navigate our life and how we give and receive love through our feelings. He helps us to govern these feelings and put them in their rightful place. Be assured they do have a place, but it's not in the driver's seat. We should not dismiss them but cultivate them through Agape Love. Feelings always come with conditions. The Holy Spirit comes without conditions.

When we have the Holy Spirit, he indicates how we are to love and receive love, not our feelings. He changes the Heart of Man to reflect the Heart of God. We know this because the Bible tells us that the Fruit of the Spirit is: love, joy, peace, patience, kindness, goodness, gentleness, faithfulness, and self-control. Those nine "fruits" are the result of having the Spirit in our lives.

The difference between being led by our feelings as

an indicator versus being led by the Spirit is the difference between loving with Agape Love which is unconditional, and "loving" with conditions that act on feelings and say or think things like: "If you are nice to me, then I'll be nice to you." "If you accept me, then I'll accept you." "If you are faithful to me, then I'll be faithful to you."

We may have an Eros love for the person we're dating, a Storge Love for our parents, or a Phileo Love for our friends, but the most excellent way to love each person in our life is through Agape Love. When Agape is our foundation of love, those other forms of love don't disappear. Instead, they are enhanced, improved upon, and made complete. They grow healthier and flourish, and we enjoy peace within them—at least as far as it depends on us.

> "If it is possible, as far as it depends on you,
> live at peace with everyone."
> -Romans 12:18 NIV

Of course, we can't control how others will love us in return, but that's okay because Agape Love is not contingent on the responses of others!

Tuning our spiritual ears to the Holy Spirit helps us

to love as we were built to love. But we need to do more than listen. We need to obey the prompting of the Spirit with our actions. He will direct us, but if we wobble in our obedience, trying to reason with why or how he's telling us to love because it seems too difficult or the other person doesn't deserve it, etc., then we diminish the voice of the Holy Spirit. Our carnal mind takes over, and before we know it, we're back to old ways of allowing our feelings to govern how and if we love.

The key to hearing and obeying the Spirit is cultivating and nurturing our walk with the Lord continuously. When we do, we give Agape Love its rightful place of reigning in our life. This means we experience God's love and fall more in love with him. When that happens, we are tuned up and tuned in to loving others with Agape Love.

My Personal Testimony: Agape Restores

I'm passionate about helping others understand this subject of love because of my experiences and how God has worked in my life. My mom gave birth to me when she was only twelve years old. I was conceived out of rape. Growing up, I loved my mom, but I couldn't understand why our relationship was the way it was...

challenging! My mother was not equipped to raise a child at her age, but, of course, I did not have the maturity or insight as a child to be able to give grace to her. Instead, I had a bad attitude for years and nursed a grudge against her. Resentment took root in my young heart and grew because I wished she was a better parent.

Later, as my relationship with God matured, he bestowed grace on me one day as I had a moment with him (in the ladies' room of all places!). He took me back in my mind to my mother's age when she was raising me. In his goodness and compassion, he opened my eyes to recognize how I had been cared for by her to the best of her ability and then reminded me of the provision I received as my grandmother took care of me. He infused compassion for my mother into my heart, and the grudge I had held onto for years started to dissolve. The Holy Spirit began to convict me and teach me the art of forgiveness!

Once I chose to forgive my mom, our relationship improved, and my Storge Love for her matured as Agape Love was now its foundation. My compassion and sympathy for her became even more profound when she told me she had been diagnosed with bipolar disorder. This reality brought forth a different behavior in me. I wasn't in the mental health field back then. If I had been, I'm sure I would have recognized her symptoms for what they meant, but, thankfully, God opened my eyes and heart to the trauma my mother must have experienced as a twelve-year-old and beyond (she was married at thirteen and had five kids by fifteen).

God also provided me with insight. My mom was ill in a debilitating way, and the Holy Spirit gave me a deeper understanding and love for her. My mom has passed on now, but I share this brief testimony to illustrate how Agape Love restores! We must love beyond feelings and love by the power of the Holy Spirit. When we do, good things happen.

Do you see? Storge Love for my mother wasn't enough to have a healthy and God-honoring relationship with her. Storge Love can be hot or cold. It is about the parent/child relationship, but it isn't unconditional like Agape Love. It doesn't forgive over and over again like Agape. It doesn't sympathize like Agape. Storge Love could not sustain me properly in my relationship with my mom. So, before I yielded to the Holy Spirit, I would love my mom "enough" to pick up the phone when she would call me, but I'd be rolling my eyes and making faces on the other end of the line because I knew she was calling to ask for money or meet a need she had and that annoyed me!

Storge Love can justify our lack of respect, generosity, and bad attitude. I needed Agape Love to govern my heart and supersede my feelings so I could love my mom with a sincere heart.

I wish a change of heart toward my mom would have developed earlier in my life, but it didn't happen until I yielded to Christ. I knew as a believer that I was required *and* equipped to have Agape Love for her. Agape is complete and is rooted in patience, forgiveness, trust, hope, etc. It never fails. Storge alone will fail us because it only goes so far. Storge Love doesn't require forgiveness, but Agape Love does. I'm grateful for that realization and how the Holy Spirit guided and helped me forgive. I'll say it again... Agape Love restores! By the grace of God, I was given the gift of Agape Love to bestow upon my mother while she was still alive on this earth.

Choosing to Love... and Sometimes Letting Go

We have choices in life, obviously. Having Agape Love through Christ doesn't mean we are robots and automatically, miraculously love others with perfect love. We are still humans and have free will, which means we have choices. Will we make the choice to love rightly and unconditionally and allow the Holy Spirit to guide us? Or, will we choose to love in our own strength or not be loving at all?

Sometimes, when we're in the thick of an Eros Love relationship and know in our spirit that something isn't right, we need to go to the Holy Spirit and ask him to make things clear and help us look beyond our feelings. A question like, *"Is this the person I should be investing my time on and partnering with?"* is wisdom. Perhaps we are dating someone who needs to address specific issues in his life before we can enter a healthy relationship. In such a case, it would be wise to utilize the gift of choice in a positive, proactive way.

If we say we are a believer but not exercising our faith (our belief in God and his ways), we open ourselves up to chaos in our relationships. But when we utilize God's love—Agape Love—above Eros, we can make the hard choice and say, "I'm going to release this person and let them go their own way. If he is willing to take a hard look at the issue, submit to God, and allow the Lord to lead him to return to the relationship, we can move forward. But if not, then the Holy Spirit may be using this situation to let us know that our relationship is not the will of God. If this is true, then we're better off without it."

I know that's not easy, and it may feel like such a scary risk, but we can trust that Agape Love will meet our needs more than any relationship outside of Christ can. Agape Love provides comfort, belonging, consistency... unconditional love. Our needs can't be met entirely by another human being, and if an Eros Love relationship outside of marriage is not God's will, then choosing to let go is the wisest and most obedient way to live.

Another thing About Feelings

Those strong "crazy-in-love" feelings that come from Eros Love die down after a while. It doesn't mean you don't love the person who is the object of your Eros Love anymore, but it needs to be accompanied by Agape Love in order to thrive and flourish for the long haul.

The same is true with our Phileo Love relationships. It's easy to be a friend when we agree on things, make similar life choices, or feel supported, but what if we're giving a hundred percent to the friendship and the other person is in a challenging season and is only giving fifty percent? How long will we carry Phileo Love for that friend? Will we feel hurt and abandon the relationship because of their actions or lack of response toward us? Phileo Love might say that is reasonable, but Agape Love goes deeper.

As our love for Christ grows, our ability to love others grows. And, if we're not "feeling" close to God or "feeling" Agape Love, we can rekindle it by spending time in God's word and with mature believers, receiving good teaching, and praying. Agape is not about the feelings and emotions we experience; it's about the unconditional nature of God's love for us. It comes with no conditions! It's always present for the one who believes in Jesus. That reality fuels us to love others with Agape Love and make right (and oftentimes difficult) choices on how to do that.

Pause and Ask Yourself:

- In what ways have I acted on my feelings this week as I've interacted with those in my life? What were some results?

- Was there a situation where I chose to love unconditionally instead of conditionally this week? If so, what was the result?

- Is God prompting me to show extra measures of love and grace to someone? Name that person.

—◆—

Action Steps: If you answered "yes" to that last question, pray and ask God to show you how to best *Agape Love* that person this week (Love is a verb, an action!). Don't wait or try and reason with God. Come up with a "love plan" and get busy loving this person now! Is God telling you to forgive them? If so, show them forgiveness. Is he telling you to provide for them? Give generously. Is God telling you to share a meal with them? Be hospitable with a sincere heart. Remember, you were built for love... to receive it *and* bestow it upon others.

Prayer: *"Dear God, help me to be aware of how and when I'm allowing my feelings to rule over my thoughts, words, and actions. I need them to be governed by you. May your Holy Spirit regenerate me so I can love others with Agape Love. Amen."*

Chapter 9

The Fullness of Love

I f you weren't familiar with the different types of love before you picked up this book, I hope you now have a solid idea of what each one looks like. You should be able to identify relationships in your life that fall into the love categories of Eros, Storge, and Phileo. And, if you're a Christian, you experienced the highest form of love when you accepted Jesus into your life Agape Love–and it's ongoing, never-ending.

If you're not a follower of Christ and would like to become a Christian, let me help you understand what that means. First, a little history lesson: Jesus' mission when he came to earth as a baby, born to the Virgin Mary, had everything to do with Agape Love. He is the Son of God, and he came not just as a nice guy and a good example but as the Messiah. He was the only One who could make atonement for the sins of the world so that each one of us can be forgiven, have a relationship with God, be filled with the Holy Spirit, and spend eternity with the triune God — Father, Son, and Holy Spirit — now and in heaven.

Jesus' time on earth was an act of sacrificial love. He left heaven to come to earth, experiencing the same challenges and human limitations we all do, even though he is God's son. As he grew up and began his ministry, many people heard him teach, witnessed his miracles, and believed him to be the Messiah, but also many did not. Some of those who refused to believe falsely accused Jesus and sought to have him killed for blasphemy. They thought they had succeeded in putting an end to him and his claims when he was crucified on a cross and buried, but death could not hold him (Acts 2:21-36)!

There were many witnesses to testify that Jesus rose from the grave. He appeared to his disciples and other followers before he ascended to heaven to sit at the right hand of God–his mission completed. What, then, is required of us? Simply to believe in Jesus and accept his gift of grace. When he returned to heaven, he sent the Holy Spirit to live in the hearts of believers. "But you will receive power when the Holy Spirit comes on you; and you will be my witnesses in Jerusalem, and in all Judea and Samaria, and to the ends of the earth..." (Acts 1:8 NIV). This power is given to help us live rightly, love unconditionally, and grow his kingdom.

Now, if we think we're good enough and Christ's death on the cross wasn't necessary for us, we must think again. Roman 3:23 (NIV) tells us, "For all have sinned, and come short of the glory of God." This sin displeases God, and there are consequences for it, but also, he made a way for us to be forever forgiven: *"For the wages of sin is death; but the gift of God is eternal life through Jesus Christ our Lord"* (*Romans* 6:23 *NIV*). The Bible tells us (Romans 3:23 NIV), "But God demonstrates His own love toward us, in that while we were still sinners, Christ died for us." Jesus' death paid the price for our sins. It was the ultimate price, paid out of ultimate love. Agape in action!

If we respond to his gracious act of Agape Love like we're told in Romans 10:9, our life and the way we love will change most wonderfully because of our salvation and God's work in our life: *"...*if you confess with your mouth Jesus as Lord, and believe in your heart that God raised Him from the dead, you will be saved."

Being "saved" means we are assured of heaven and

much more. We are assured of a relationship with the Triune God–Father, Son, and Holy Spirit. We are assured of God's Agape Love for all eternity. We are adopted into his family and reap the benefits of God's ultimate sacrifice for the world–his ultimate act of Agape Love! Once we accept Jesus as our Lord and Savior, we can live and operate in the fullness of that love. We may experience and exercise Eros, Storge, and Phileo Love, but we can live in the power of Agape Love and love others unconditionally.

Will we be perfect 100% of the time? No, I'm afraid not. Our humanness will certainly get in the way, but as Christians, we do have the power available to us. And, hopefully, more often than not, being motivated by God's love for us, we will choose to draw on that power.

Unconditional Means Unconditional!

"Unconditional" is a big word, not because it comprises thirteen letters, but because of its definition. Merriam-Webster defines it as *"Not conditional or limited."* So, if God's love is unconditional, which it is, there is nothing we can do to cause him to love us more or love us less. We can't earn his love because we are especially good or perfect. And we can't lose it because we've somehow blown it (again). His love is about who *he* is, not what *we are* or what we *do*. We don't have to get our act together for him to love us.

This doesn't mean that there are no consequences for our choices in life, but nothing that we do and nothing that happens to us can separate us from the love of God (Romans 8:38-39 AMP).

> For I am convinced [and continue to be convinced— beyond any doubt] that neither death, nor life, nor angels, nor principalities, nor things present and threatening, nor things to come, nor powers, nor height, nor depth, nor any other created thing, will be able to separate us from the [unlimited] love of God, which is in Christ Jesus our Lord.

Take in those verses for a few minutes, like soaking up the sun after days of clouds and rain. Do you feel their warmth? God gave us those verses in the Bible so we would know how far-reaching and powerful his love is, but words can't fully express the love God has for us. No word is adequate! We can't fully understand it; we just have to accept it. No one is left out, but in order to live in and experience his unconditional love, we have to make Jesus our Lord and Savior.

We also must remember, day after day, that unconditional means unconditional. Unlimited means unlimited — we can do nothing to detour God's unconditional love away from us. It is constant, consistent, and without boundaries. Even if we were to walk away from him and reject his love, his love remains intact. No other form of love (Eros, Storge, Phileo) fulfills that hole in us to be loved unconditionally. Agape Love is the only one.

Be aware that Satan wants us to doubt and live as if Agape Love is not true. He seeks to sabotage and pollute the reality of God's Word and his promises. We must turn a deaf ear to Satan's hisses of accusation, like, "You blew it again. Now God is angry with you and doesn't love you." Or "You've used up your forgiveness." Or, when things don't go your way, "God is punishing you, and you are no longer in his love." These are lies. They go against the Word of God.

When we live in God's unconditional love, it changes everything! We can love others in a way that is beyond us, yet not beyond God. We can now truly love others with Agape Love because God loved us first, and with that comes so much freedom! The Bible tells us that "Now the Lord is the Spirit, and where the Spirit of the Lord is, there is liberty [emancipation from bondage, true freedom]" (2 Corinthians 3:17 AMP). Because of his unconditional love for us and with the help of the Holy Spirit, we are free to truly love others with a love that not only enhances but supersedes Eros, Storge, and Phileo Love.

And when others don't love us as we wish they would, we don't need to be devastated because God's love covers us. So, when that husband doesn't love us exactly as we want him to, we gotta run back to Agape Love! When romantic love falls short (and it will), we gotta run back to God's love because it fulfills. When a friend disappoints us, we can live in peace because we know our true satisfaction is found in Christ. When our sister makes a hurtful comment, we can forgive because Christ loves us and forgives our every offense. His unconditional love is always available and reliable toward us and in helping us love others.

If we give Agape Love its place of reigning in our lives, we could change the world right where we live! Allowing Agape Love to govern our actions will give us a heart for the people in our lives that we may first think we don't need to love or are loving "well enough." Yet when God gets ahold of us, and we experience regeneration through the Holy Spirit, we will seek out those he nudges us to love and love them well. We would be wise to make Agape Love the foundation of all our Eros,

Storge, and Phileo relationships. Marriage is a ministry. Our family relationships and friendships are ministry, too.

As for loving the rest of the world, look at who is already in your sphere of influence. It's wonderful to send money to help fund charities' work to feed the poor or rescue people from sex trafficking. It's important to support causes that fight racial injustice, and I encourage you to participate in loving the world in these ways. They are effective practices for loving our fellow man. Still, there are plenty of "organic" opportunities to love others on a regular or daily basis that are outside of our family and friends are significant. However, you won't receive a tax deduction!

For example, if you are a barista, love your customers by smiling at them and showing them patience when they are overly demanding or grumpy. If you are a teacher, love your students by being kind to them, being prepared each day to teach them well, and praying for them. If you are a company CEO, treat your employees and peers with respect and give them the benefit of the doubt when issues arise...you get the idea.

Here is an example of loving the world (those within my sphere of influence) from my own life: As a therapist, I come into my office every day, and while my practice is founded on Christian principles as I am a believer, I meet with clients who are a mix of believers and nonbelievers (those who follow a different faith or who are agnostic or atheist). Yet, no matter where they land spiritually, each client trusts me to speak into their lives, encourage them, lead them in therapeutic modalities, or give them Scripture that has proven true in my life and that I know will have power in their life.

As I meet with these different people, I must put aside my biases and engage with them out of the Fruit of the Spirit (love, joy, peace, patience, kindness, goodness, faithfulness, gentleness, and self-control), whether they have a relationship with the Lord or not. In doing this, I seek to love each one of my clients and help them navigate whatever they are struggling with regarding their mental and emotional health.

I must make a conscious choice as I meet with them to practice an unconditional, Agape "love walk" every day. This choice extends to everyone–those who don't serve the God I serve and worship the God I worship and those who do.

As I help each client, I'm committed to respecting their brokenness and working with them through it without judgment because that's what Agape Love does. God has also nudged me at times to provide this service for free to those who don't have the money to pay me. In these cases, my commitment stands–to bestow on them the same Agape Love in how I help them because I know that's what God wants from me, and I can trust him to meet my own financial needs.

My conviction and ultimate motivation to serve with love those I counsel comes from Jesus–the one I love and who loves me!

Pause and Ask Yourself:

- How does the life, death, and resurrection of Jesus make a difference in your life?

- How does it empower you to live *in* Agape love and love others *with* Agape love?

- Who is in your sphere of influence beyond your family that you can love? How will you do that?

Action Steps:

- If you made a first-time confession of faith, believing Jesus to be your Savior, tell someone you know and trust. They may or may not be able to relate to you, but verbalizing your decision is a first step toward owning your faith and living in it.

- If you've known and followed Christ for a while, tell someone about what this means in your life. Your testimony may encourage them to make a decision for Christ and live in Agape Love.

Prayer: *"Heavenly Father, thank you for sending your Son, Jesus, as payment for my sins. Help me live in the truth of your unconditional love and bless others by loving them with you in mind. Amen."*

Chapter 10

Take it Step by Step

1 Corinthians 13 is one of those chapters in the Bible we must regularly revisit, not only because it is powerful and essential to our lives today, but because we have short memories and must be reminded often! So, I'm concluding this book by having us look at this passage again—this time, going through it thoroughly verse by verse.

While Scripture is clear that we are not to take away from God's Word nor add to it, I want to share what I call "food for thought" and break down verses one to thirteen (in the Amplified Bible version) in bite-sized chunks. I hope this will help you remember these verses, take them to heart, and effectively put them into practice.

The Excellence of Love

> If I speak with the tongues of men and of angels but
> have not love [for others growing out of God's Love
> for me], then I have become only a noisy gong or a
> clanging cymbal [just an annoying distraction].

Verse one of chapter 13 tells us that love is paramount.
Whatever we do as humans that is commendable, it
matters very little if we do not have love. Without acting
in love, we allow ourselves to get in the way of God's
plan. It doesn't matter what language we speak.
Whether it's a "natural" language or of the Spirit, Agape
Love must be its base; otherwise, we're not loving with
God's love. We are merely a distraction from God's
ways through our words or actions toward others.

> And if I have the gift of prophecy [and speak a new
> message from God to the people], and understand
> all mysteries, and [possess] all knowledge; and if I
> have all [sufficient] faith so that I can remove moun-
> tains, but do not have Love [reaching out to others], I
> am nothing.

No matter what gifts God has given us and how

they look to others, we are nothing without the truth of love. We can share all kinds of great knowledge and even revelation about the amazing plans God has for us and others, but if we don't love with God's love, we are nothing (though we may find it hard to understand, we are nothing without the true love of Christ). If we believe God's word is above all else and nothing but the truth, that is our final answer: we must have love.

> If I give all my possessions to feed the poor, and if I surrender my body to be burned, but do not have Love, it does me no good at all.

It does not matter how much money we use to do acts of service for others or what size check we put into the offering plate if we don't give out of love. These acts don't gain us points or make us great at love. They create no good toward a more excellent way of love in and of themselves. It looks appealing to give of oneself, but if giving of ourselves is not driven from a place of unselfishness, it does us no good.

> Love endures with patience and serenity, Love is kind and thoughtful, and is not jealous or envious; Love does not brag and is not proud or arrogant.

Love has a way of showing itself through patience and thoughtfulness, in thinking about others without any other motive except for love. It does not look upon what others have with a spirit of jealousy or envy. It praises others for who they are and celebrates what opportunities or possessions they have obtained instead of wishing we were in their shoes. Real love does not go around talking about everything we get, bragging about it, or displaying a self-righteous attitude. When we think and behave like it's all about us, we showcase self-centeredness, not love. Practicing to improve how we think about love will help us be in the moment with others, take action in life, and demonstrate love.

> It is not rude; it is not self-seeking, it is not provoked [nor overly sensitive and easily angered]; it does not take into account a wrong endured.

When our thoughts and actions have more to do with looking out for ourselves than others, we are not practicing love. When we are focused on ourselves, it's all too easy to make excuses or feel justified as to why we've acted rudely toward others. Also, love assumes the best about someone else. We don't always know the battles people are fighting in their life, the struggles they are going through. We must be willing to forgive quickly and process our feelings to remain in pure love.

"It does not rejoice at injustice, but rejoices with the truth [when right and truth prevail].

Love celebrates the truth about what is right and fights for connection, not disconnection. Injustice separates people and only promotes more unjust behaviors. When we rejoice when things do not go right for others, we are arrogant and behave unjustly, which is not the way of love.

Love bears all things [regardless of what comes], believes all things [looking for the best in each one], hopes all things [remaining steadfast during difficult times], endures all things [without weakening].

Love is solid and durable and has the strength to fight for good no matter what happens. The foundation of love is built on truth, so it believes the best about others and life itself. Sometimes we want to give in to weakness but remember to remain strong because love does not faint. Even when things become complicated, and they sometimes do, love does not easily give up.

Love is tough... in a good way! There is a saying, "When life gives you lemons, make lemonade." I would add, "And don't forget to add love–your sweetener!"

> Love never fails [it never fades nor ends]. But as for prophecies, they will pass away; as for tongues, they will cease; as for the gift of special knowledge, it will pass away.

We fall short of loving others when we don't submit to the never-failing, never giving-up-on-anyone nature of true love. Real love supports the "No man left behind" mandate. Love never fails us or others. Various things, situations, and people will come and go, but not true love. It is not based on whims, feelings, or passing fancies. Love is rock-solid, intent on benefiting others, regardless of the cost. God's love never fails and never ends—it continues through all eternity.

> For we know in part, and we prophesy in part [for our knowledge is fragmentary and incomplete].

As a counselor, I often interact with people who aren't seeing the full picture of what is happening in their lives. They lack an essential element of understanding or insight into a particular issue in their life. When I think about the fragmentation of our thinking, it can consist of small parts that are disconnected or incomplete in processing. The same is true regarding our thoughts about God. We would be wise to remember that we don't know everything about God and need his Spirit to make intercession for us. So let the Spirit speak! Ask him to intercede on your behalf because he possesses a complete understanding of all things.

> But when that which is complete and perfect comes,
> that which is incomplete and partial will pass away.

We worry about so many things during our lifetime. If only we would allow God to do his excellent work within our life, our worries would dissipate. Only one thing lasts God's perfect love.

> When I was a child, I talked like a child, I thought
> like a child, I reasoned like a child; when I became a
> man, I did away with childish things.

When we allow maturity to take its place in our lives, we grow and develop into the sons (and daughters) of God we were made to be, taking ownership of our thoughts and behavior.

> For now [in this time of imperfection] we see in a mirror dimly [a blurred reflection, a riddle, an enigma], but then [when the time of perfection comes we will see reality] face to face. Now I know in part [just in fragments], but then I will know fully, just as I have been fully known [by God].

On this side of heaven, we will not be perfect! But we can live daily experiencing and viewing who we want to become through God's Word. We can also be confident of the promise we find in Philippians 1:6 (AMP), which says, "...He who began a good work in you will [continue to] perfect and complete it until the day of Christ Jesus [the time of His return]."

We must challenge the world telling us who we are through television, movies, social media, etc. In reality, we are who God says we are, based on his unconditional love for us. We are his beloved.

> And now there remain: faith [abiding trust in God and His promises], hope [confident expectation of eternal salvation], Love [unselfish Love for others

growing out of God's Love for me], these three [the choicest graces]; but the greatest of these is Love.

Let us trust the Lord of our lives and his unconditional love for us. We can only walk this "love walk" as we take that truth to heart and learn to love ourselves and those around us in the power of the Holy Spirit and Jesus' Name.

Pause and Ask Yourself

What attribute of love is God calling me to work on?

—❤—

Action Step: On the pages that follow, there are five questions that will help you assess for your knowledge and thoughts regarding love, as well as any new insight you have gained. Answer the questions and allow these revelations, thoughts, and insights to assist you into the next level of your "love walk."

Answer Key can be found
at the end of the quiz.

Prayer: *"Heavenly Father, help me to take your Word to heart, to meditate on it, and act on it. Help me love others well and in the way you designed love to be and fully accept your love for me. Amen."*

The Purpose of Love

1. What are some of the attributes or outcomes of love according to the Excellence of Love verses?

    a. thoughtfulness, perseverance, hope
    b. encouragement, kindness, praise
    c. endurance, growth, refinement
    d. all the above

2. Love is primarily for the:

    a. past
    b. present
    c. future
    d. all the above

3. The goal of love is to instill God's way for changes in us through our:

    a. thoughts
    b. emotions
    c. behavior
    d. all the above

4. The world's way of love can be hypersensitive to any action or response viewed as negative.

    a. True
    b. False

5. It is possible for us to change our negative bias when we submit to Agape Love and allow the Holy Spirit to help us love others.

    a. True
    b. False

Answers: 1. D, 2. D, 3. D, 4. A, 5. A.

I hope this helps you further evaluate your "love walk" according to God's word. Where do you see issues? What does it prompt you to address in your life?

Take these things to the Lord, ask him to help you experience his Agape Love, and generously bestow it upon others. After all, you, me, the person sitting next to you at church, and the guy in the car behind you were all *built for love!*

Let us live life out how we were made to live it... with Agape Love at its foundation.

About the Author

Casandra Merritt is the CEO and Owner of *Start Fresh Counseling Center* in Brandon, Florida. She is also a Certified Behavioral Health Case Manager Supervisor and a practicing Christian Family Therapist.

She has a Bachelor of Science in Human Services with a Concentration in Early Childhood Education and a Master's in Mental Health Counseling. In addition, she holds a post-Master's in counseling in Play Therapy, and is currently attending Liberty University to complete her doctorate.

Casandra conducts training, hosts, and speaks at various conferences. She was selected for inclusion in the Trademark Women of Distinction Honors Edition. She also serves as an Assistant Pastor at her local church and believes her assignment on earth is to make known Jesus Christ's mystery of man's will and integrate mental health counseling to uncover one's true potential, leading to a life worth celebrating.

Bibliography

BibleGateway.com: A searchable online Bible in over 150 versions and 50 languages. (2022, June 1)

BibleGateway.Com: A Searchable Online Bible in over 150 Versions and 50 Languages.; The Zondervan Corporation. http://biblegateway.com

Casandra Merritt, CEO, MS, MHC 2022

Chapman, G. (2014). *The 5 Love Languages.* Moody Publishers.

Merriam-Webster. (2022). *The Merriam-Webster Dictionary.*

Walt Disney. (1942)